Horatio Adams

An Address delivered before the Massachusetts Medical Society at the Annual Meeting, May 26, 1858

SALZWASSER
VERLAG

Horatio Adams

An Address delivered before the Massachusetts Medical Society at the Annual Meeting, May 26, 1858

Reprint of the original, first published in 1859.

1st Edition 2022 | ISBN: 978-3-37513-150-0

Verlag (Publisher): Salzwasser Verlag GmbH, Zeilweg 44, 60439 Frankfurt, Deutschland
Vertretungsberechtigt (Authorized to represent): E. Roepke, Zeilweg 44, 60439 Frankfurt, Deutschland
Druck (Print): Books on Demand GmbH, In de Tarpen 42, 22848 Norderstedt, Deutschland

AN

ADDRESS

DELIVERED BEFORE THE

MASSACHUSETTS MEDICAL SOCIETY,

AT THE

ANNUAL MEETING,

May 26, 1858.

By HORATIO ADAMS, M.D.

OF WALTHAM.

BOSTON:

PRINTED BY DAVID CLAPP.

MEDICAL AND SURGICAL JOURNAL OFFICE.

1858.

INVESTIGATIONS

UPON THE

SUBJECT OF VACCINATION.

BY HORATIO ADAMS, M.D.
OF WALTHAM.

READ AT THE ANNUAL MEETING, MAY 26, 1858.

MR. PRESIDENT AND FELLOWS OF THE SOCIETY:

IN accordance with our time-honored custom, we are assembled here to-day, from all parts of our Commonwealth, to celebrate the anniversary of this our cherished Society, to perpetuate its existence, and, if possible, extend its boundaries, that its beneficent influences may be more widely felt and enjoyed, — to lay aside our professional toils and duties, to renew our acquaintance, to indulge in the expression and interchange of kindly and social feelings ; in a word, to keep bright that chain of friendship which binds us together, and makes us not only happier, but better men and better physicians. It gives me pleasure to extend to you a cordial and affectionate welcome.

The sources of professional information are two-fold. The one is contained in the writings of our predecessors, and requires the student's first attention. The other is our own careful and well-

30

considered observations, which may be termed the clinical part of the physician's education. It is here he acquires a practical acquaintance with the natural history of diseases. The importance of this branch of medical education cannot be over-estimated. But if the student, I may say the physician, (for he must always be a student), has not already acquired a knowledge of the various departments of medical science, embraced in the medical literature of our predecessors, he will be incompetent to understand the teachings which the bed-side would otherwise unfold to him. It has been wisely said, that "he who does not profit by the experience of the past, must always remain in his infancy." To no subject is this remark more applicable than to the science of medicine. What could we now know of this science, if the teachings of the past had not been made our own?

We certainly owe our predecessors a debt of gratitude for the copious means of knowledge which they have transmitted to us. Have we not, then, on our part, a duty to perform to those who are to succeed us? Shall we simply hand down to them what has been so liberally bequeathed to us? or shall we add to it, and give to it the impress of our own times? I conceive it to be the bounden duty of each one of us, to do the little that in him lies to extend the boundaries of medical science. This result cannot be attained without the untiring and successive labors of the many. The experience of no one man, however extensive it may be, is alone sufficient to accomplish, to any great extent, so important an object. Yet each one can do something. His investigations, if properly conducted, will make some addition to the accumulating mass. If he would diligently and accurately investigate some one subject, the result, small though it may appear to him, would, nevertheless, add to the increasing aggregate.

It is this conviction, gentlemen, that we should all be co-workers in the accumulation of knowledge, rather than any conscious fitness or ability to lay before you any thing new, or essentially to advance our knowledge of medical science, that has impelled me to accept the honorable position, which the kindness of your officers has assigned to me for this hour.

In carrying out this conviction, I must solicit your indulgence, while I lay before you some of the results of my investigations upon the subject of Vaccination.*

The history of the discovery of vaccination, which had its origin about sixty years ago, is too familiar to you to require any notice at this time. A recital also of the zeal, industry and patient scientific research, which the immortal Jenner exhibited in connection with its discovery, of the calumny he endured, of the opposition he encountered not only among the common people, but to some extent in the profession also, and of the triumphant success which crowned his untiring efforts, would be to repeat an oft-told tale, and could add nothing to his well-

* Some of the statistics embraced in this discourse were used as the basis of a short address read before the Middlesex South District Medical Society, in April, 1857.

earned and universally acknowledged fame. The gratitude of the profession, not of his own country alone, nor of any one country, but of the entire civilized world, for this great boon to the human family, has been recently most signally expressed, by the erection in London of a bronze statue* to his memory. We hazard nothing, I think, in saying that the wish of every member of the profession who has contributed so cheerfully to this object, is, that this their testimony of respect and gratitude may be enduring as the benefit he has conferred on our race.

It cannot be denied that, within the last thirty years, public confidence has been somewhat shaken, at least in the permanency of the prophylactic power of vaccination, if not in its general efficacy as a protection against the ravages of small-pox. At the commencement of this period (1825 to 1830), the public, and, to a certain extent, the profession also, seemed fully to realize that all were not perfectly protected by it; and subsequently, this feeling was somewhat confirmed by the prevalence, I may say the epidemic prevalence, of small-pox in New England from about 1835 to 1845 ; during which period, many persons, who had been vaccinated, contracted the disease. The scepticism so prevalent at that time has not yet been entirely removed. Nevertheless, there is no question that vaccination has afforded, and still affords, complete protection to a

---

* This statue, erected by the voluntary subscription of the profession, no one being allowed to contribute more than one dollar, has been, we understand, completed within the last few weeks.

very large majority of those who have been subject-
ed to its influence, and comparative protection and
almost absolute exemption from death by small-pox
to all. At the same time, it must be admitted that
the operation has, in some few instances, been of no
avail. Dr. Jenner early discovered this fact. This,
instead of discouraging us, should make us the more
desirous of ascertaining the causes of failure, that
we may be able to extend to the entire human family the unquestionable benefits enjoyed by far the
greater proportion of it. A candid and careful investigation of the subject may perhaps serve to elu-
cidate some points which may have been involved
in uncertainty, and possibly aid us in determining
how far the occasional failures are to be attributed
to imperfection in the agent itself, and how far to
the mode in which it has been applied ; to changes
which time may have wrought in its character, and
to carelessness, ignorance or neglect in its application. This should also be done for the purpose, if
possible, of satisfying the public mind, and restoring
that confidence in the protective power of the disease, so essential to its universal application.

It is frequently alleged that the number of instances of small-pox occurring after vaccination is
proportionally greater now than formerly. Let us
inquire carefully into the causes usually assigned
for this increased failure in the protective power of
the vaccine disease, in order to determine whether
there is any foundation for the opinion, so generally
entertained, that the disease has lost something of
its protective energy ; and then, if possible, point

out a remedy for the evil, so far as it shall be found to exist.

The causes usually assigned for the occasional failure of the vaccine disease to protect against the infection of small-pox, may be summed up under three heads.

1st, That, after a longer or shorter interval, it exerts but a very feeble if any protective influence over the system, and consequently a renewed susceptibility to small-pox infection ensues.

2d, That the stock of vaccine virus in use has become deteriorated, in consequence of its frequent transmission through the human body.   And,

3d, That the operation of vaccination is not always properly performed ; that virus is taken at an improper time, or from an imperfectly developed vesicle, or is inserted into the arms of those who are otherwise so far diseased as to prevent its proper development.

The first question is, does the vaccine disease, after an interval of longer or shorter duration, lose any of its protective influence over the system, and is the susceptibility to small-pox infection consequently increased ?

The theory that the protective power of the vaccine disease is eliminated by time, is, I think, maintained by many able practitioners of medicine. Other distinguished physicians indirectly admit the same theory, by recommending a re-vaccination at certain stated periods.   Among the more distinguished of the former, are Drs. Brown, Munro, Thomas and Copeland ; among the latter may be named Drs. Stewart, Forry, Shaffer, Losetti, and many others.

If this theory be true, the vaccine disease forms an exception to the rule applicable to all other diseases which are capable of being produced only once in the same person, as measles, scarlet fever, chicken-pox, &c. If these diseases are ever produced a second time in the same individual, it is an exception to the rule. Nevertheless, such cases do sometimes occur. So with variola, it does sometimes appear a second time in the same person ; and statistics go to show that its second appearance, in some of its modified forms, is relatively about as frequent as the occurrence of the same disease after a well ascertained case of vaccination. In settling questions of this nature, however, we must rely only on well ascertained facts.

It may be well to remark, at this stage of our discussion, that it is well settled by medical experience, that a second vaccination is as good a test as small-pox inoculation, to decide whether a patient is perfectly protected from small-pox infection.

If time gradually eliminates from the system the prophylactic power of the vaccine disease, we must expect to see the susceptibility to it under a re-vaccination increased in exact proportion to that elimination ; in other words, the greater the length of time which has elapsed since the first vaccination, the nearer will be the approach to a perfect vesicle under a re-vaccination.

In order to show the facts on this point, I must ask your attention to a series of observations which

have been made with great care. The results I believe to be perfectly reliable.

Several years since, the writer vaccinated all the
persons at that time in the employment of the Boston Manufacturing Company, in Waltham, num-
bering between five and six hundred. About
this period there was considerable excitement in
consequence of the prevalence of small-pox —
several cases having indeed occurred in that vil-
lage. Consequently none were opposed to receiv-
ing the additional protection which a re-vaccination might give them; and little or no objection
was made to the accomplishment of the object.

Directly from the arm of a healthy child, on the
eighth day of the disease, I vaccinated, at each time,
as many as could be conveniently examined on the
subsequent third, fifth, eighth and tenth days. Vac-
cinating with recent virus, I rarely failed to have it
take effect. At the same time, a record was made
of the name of each person vaccinated, and also the
date of his previous vaccination. This date could
not always be ascertained with certainty. Some in-
dividuals could not remember when they were first
vaccinated; but they could remember whether it
was done in childhood or at a later period. By
ascertaining the age, an approximation to the truth
could always be made. The variations, if any, would
be as likely to occur in one direction as the other.
The appearances of each case were carefully noted
down at the time of making the examinations, on
the several days above indicated. The whole number of cases vaccinated was 579; of this number 89

had never been vaccinated. At the present time I shall use the recorded cases of those only who had previously received vaccination.

The facts and observations thus obtained, have been arranged in a tabular form, as follows. First, I ascertained the number of persons who had been previously vaccinated in each year, up to twenty-five years, which was the longest time that had elapsed since any one had had the operation performed. In the next place, the appearances of each case were carried into the table as they were noted down on the third, fifth, eighth and tenth days. The table will be read thus: six cases had been vaccinated one year; six of them inflamed on or before the third day, and a vesicle had begun to form on two of them; on the fifth day a yellow vesicle was formed in four cases, and a crust had matured in two; and a pointed crust had formed on the eighth day in two cases, and also in two cases on tenth day. The table goes on in like manner with all the cases in each year. [See next page.]

TABLE I.*

No. of Cases in each year.	No. of years since first Vaccination.	Third Day.		Fifth Day.		Eighth Day.			Tenth Day.	
		Vaccinated point inflamed.	Pointed Vesicle form'd.	Yellowish pointed Vesicle formed.	Crust formed, Inflammation gone.	Vesic. large, pointed; Inflammation diffused, rough and irreg.	Vesicles flat, centre depressed.	Crust formed, Inflammation gone.	Crust forming, Inflammation around it diffused and rough.	Areola forming, Vesicle flat, Crust forming in centre.
6	1	6	2	4	2	2	...	2	2	...
8	2	8	2	6	2	...	...	6	...	...
16	3	14	12	12	10	...	...	6	...	...
10	4	10	6	6	4	...	...	6	...	...
8	5	8	4	2	6	2	...	...	2	...
24	6	22	14	4	20	...	...	4	...	...
10	7	8	6	6	2	1	1	6	1	1
30	8	30	14	10	16	2	2	10	2	2
34	9	32	16	16	14	2	2	16	2	2
104	10	100	46	34	48	4	6	46	4	6
56	11	52	28	38	30	.4	2	20	4	2
30	12	29	8	29	20	...	1	9	...	1
32	13	28	12	20	16	3	1	12	3	1
16	14	15	4	8	10	...	1	5	...	1
34	15	32	14	18	18	2	...	14	2	...
10	16	10	4	8	6	...	...	4	...	...
...	17	...	...	...	...	...	...	...	...	...
10	18	9	4	6	6	1	1	2	1	1
2	19	2	2	...	2	...	...	...	...	...
24	20	22	10	20	12	1	1	10	1	1
6	21	4	1	...	3	1	...	2	1	...
2	22	2	...	...	1	...	...	1	...	...
4	23	4	...	3	2	...	...	2	...	...
2	24	2	...	2	1	...	...	1	...	...
12	25	11	2	8	6	1	...	5	1	...
490										

From the first table a second has been formed, showing the percentage of cases in each year terminating on each of the days therein indicated. In this

* I have introduced into the above Table the entire record, as taken down at the time the observations were made — a portion only of which is used in this discourse.

table the disease is considered as having ended when the crust was formed, although inflammation, in some instances, still existed, but was declining.

The table is to be read thus: six cases had been vaccinated one year, 33·33 per cent. terminating on or before the fifth day; 33·33 per cent. on or before the eighth day; and 33·33 per cent. on or before the tenth day, with inflammation around the crust, diffused and rough; and so on with all the cases in each succeeding year.

TABLE II.

No. of Cases.	No. of years since first Vaccination.	Percentage of Cases terminating on or before 6th day.	Percentage of Cases terminating on or before 8th day.	Percentage of Cases terminating on or before 10th day, with Inflammation around Crust, diffused, irregular in form, and rough.	Percentage of Cases terminating on 10th day, with a flat Vesicle and regular Areola, and Crust beginning to form.
6	1	33·33	33·33	33·33	....
8	2	25	75	....	....
16	3	62·50	37·50	....	....
10	4	40	60	....	....
8	5	75	25	....	....
24	6	83·33	16·66	....	....
10	7	20	60	10	10
30	8	53·33	33·33	6·66	6·66
34	9	41·15	47·05	5·88	5·88
104	10	46·15	44·24	3·84	5·77
56	11	53·57	35·71	7·14	3·57
30	12	66·66	30	....	3·33
32	13	50	37·50	9·37	3·12
16	14	62·50	31·25	....	6·25
34	15	52·94	41·17	5·88	....
10	16	60	40	....	....
...	17	....	....	....	....
10	18	60	20	10	10
2	19	100	....	....	....
24	20	50	41·66	4·16	4·16
6	21	50	33·33	16·66	....
2	22	50	50	....	....
4	23	50	50	....	....
2	24	50	50	....	....
12	25	50	41·66	8·33	....

To show concisely what changes have taken place in the protective power of the vaccine disease, within the space of twenty-five years, a third table has been prepared, in which the cases have been arranged in quinquennial divisions, so as to present at a glance the number of cases in each division terminating on the several days therein indicated. Those terminating on the tenth day, are arranged in this, as in the last table, in two divisions (in the fifth and sixth columns), showing in the fifth column, those which, although passing on to the tenth day, did not present the appearances of the true disease. The sixth column shows the number that did present most of the characteristics of the true disease. The table is to be read thus : — 48 cases had been vaccinated from one to five years ; 50 per cent. of those terminated on or before the fifth day : 41·70 per cent. on the eighth day, and 8·33 per cent. on the tenth day in the fifth column ; and nothing is registered in the sixth column, or second division of cases, that extended to the tenth day ; and so on.

TABLE III.

No. of Cases.	No. of years since first Vaccination.	Percentage terminating on or before 5th day.	Percentage terminating on or before 8th day.	Percentage terminating on or before 10th day, with inflamed surface around Crust, rough and irregular.	Percentage terminating on 10th day with a flat Vesicle, Areola and Crust beginning to form.
48	1 to 5	50	41·70	8·33	....
202	5 to 10	49·50	40·59	4·45	5·44
168	10 to 15	55·95	35·71	5·35	2·97
46	15 to 20	56·52	34·78	4·34	4·34
26	20 to 25	50	42·30	7·69	....
490	....	52·45	38·57	5·30	3·67

By the last table it appears that, in the aggregate, 52.45 per cent. terminated on or before the fifth day after vaccination; 38·57 per cent. on or before the eighth day, and 5·30 per cent. on the tenth day, with inflamed surface around crust, rough and irregular; and 3·67 per cent. with a flat vesicle and an areola beginning to form. In the details, it also appears, that of those who had been previously vaccinated from one to five years, 8·33 per cent. had an irregular termination on tenth day; of those who had been previously vaccinated from five to ten years, 4·45 per cent. terminated irregularly on tenth day, and 5·44 per cent. on the same day, presenting the usual appearances of the true disease; of those vaccinated from ten to fifteen years, 5·35 per cent. had an irregular termination on tenth day, and 2·97 per cent. on the same day, with the regular appearances of the true disease; of those whose vaccination dated from fifteen to twenty years, 4·34 per cent. had an irregular termination on tenth day, and the same per cent. terminated on the same day, developing the outward appearances of the true disease; while 7·69 per cent. of those who had been vaccinated from twenty to twenty-five years, terminated on tenth day, but did not develope the characteristics of the vaccine disease.

In these tables I consider the susceptibility to the disease is indicated by the length of time which elapses, in each particular case, between the time of vaccination and the crusting of the vesicle. For instance, if the vesicle terminates on the fifth day, the individual shows much *less* susceptibility to the disease, than he would do if the vesicle should pass on to the tenth day, before arriving at maturity.

Thus it appears that of all the persons who underwent a second vaccination, less than nine per cent. seemed to show, as to the time of development, any great approach to the true disease. And those who had been vaccinated from twenty to twenty-five years, did not show so large a percentage running on to the tenth day, as was shown by those who had only been vaccinated from one to five years. The least susceptibility seems actually to have existed among those whose vaccination was the most remote.

The same general fact has been observed by others. Dr. Otto, a German physician, in a paper entitled, " Remarks on Small-pox, Vaccination, &c.," says, that " of one hundred and eighty-nine persons who underwent vaccination a second time, twenty-one only seemed to give evidence of any great susceptibility to the disease," — about 11 per cent. The same author further remarks, that " the smallest number of these is actually of those in whom the first vaccination was least recent."

It appears, then, that the facts which have been adduced do not sustain the theory of the gradual elimination, by time, of the protective influence of the vaccine disease. On the contrary, they conclusively show that the susceptibility to the disease, under a second vaccination, is not greater at the end of twenty-five years, than it is at the end of one year.

The second theory advanced, to account for the recent more frequent failure of the vaccine process to protect the system against small-pox infection, is that the virus now in use has become deteriorated, in consequence of its frequent transmission through human bodies.

No sufficient proof has ever been brought forward to establish the truth of this theory. Neither has it ever been satisfactorily shown, that the susceptibility to small-pox infection is any greater among those who have been recently vaccinated, than it is among those who underwent the operation half a century ago. Considerable difference of theoretical opinion, however, prevails upon this point; — some contending that the transit of the vaccine lymph through successive subjects does materially diminish its prophylactic power, while others, on the contrary, maintain that by transmitting the virus through a series of well predisposed children, carefully selected, it can be restored from an imperfect to a perfect state, and, with proper care, it can be retained indefinitely in that condition. We shall hereafter show, that from want of proper attention in the selection of suitable subjects to vaccinate, and proper vesicles from which to take virus, it may be, and doubtless often is, very much deteriorated. So far as we have been able to observe, if the lymph has been properly selected, and due care exercised in the choice of the person to be vaccinated, the vesicle has the same general and specific appearance now that it had thirty years ago. And the constitutional affection is believed to be as great now as it was then.

The foregoing tables conclusively prove that the

virus has not been enfeebled in consequence of its frequent transmission through human bodies, for they show that those who have been vaccinated but one year were not materially more susceptible to the disease, under a re-vaccination, than those were who had undergone the operation twenty-five years before.

M. Bousquet* maintains that " by comparing the true vesicles, which we observe after vaccination in the present day, with the descriptions and drawings left us by the original authors, it will afford results not at all favorable to the notion of the degeneration of the vaccine virus, in consequence of its repeated transmissions through human bodies; " and " on the whole," he continues, " there is no good reason for the opinion that the vaccine virus has lost any of its properties." But if, in its repeated transmissions through the human body, it has lost power, or suffered certain deteriorations impairing its original efficacy, it should not, if it were true, be urged as an objection to vaccination, since it can be so readily reproduced in all its original vigor.

The fact is probably familiar to all, that within the last twenty years it has been shown that the cow-pox can be produced by inoculating the cow with variolous matter. In the October number of the British and Foreign Med. Review, for 1839, may be found an account of Mr. Ceeley's experiment of inoculating the cow. Soon after this, in conversation with a gentleman, whom, in the words of

* In a Report made to the French Government.

another, I am privileged also to call my teacher, my physician, my friend, JAMES JACKSON, it was arranged that the writer should repeat Mr. Ceeley's experiment as soon as pure small-pox matter for the purpose could be procured. A brief account of this experiment, the first, it is believed, that was ever performed in this country with successful results, may not be out of place here.

On the 11th of January, 1840, I made several punctures with the point of a lancet under the cuticle on the right labium pudendi of two different cows; none of the punctures were sufficiently deep to draw blood. Into each of them was introduced a pointed quill well deluged with variolous matter, and allowed to remain for half an hour.

On 15th, the punctures were barely visible, but not apparently inflamed.

On 16th, two of the punctures made on the youngest cow were more distinctly visible; in drawing the finger over them, a slight hardness was felt. None of the other punctures had inflamed.

17th. These two punctures were more inflamed and a little raised, showing a pearly white, flat top, rather small.

18th. Punctures larger than yesterday, and each capped with a pearly white, flat vesicle, with centre depressed.

19th. The punctures (now vesicles) are enlarged, centres depressed.

20th. Each of the vesicles is nearly four lines in diameter; surface pearly white, flat, with centres depressed, areola not formed, slight crust in centre.

32

This P.M., end of ninth day of disease, punctured one of the vesicles; found cuticle thick, spongy and breaking, like what is seen when a vaccine vesicle is early punctured on the arm. Vesicle distinctly cellular. Transparent lymph oozed from the opening, with which I charged twenty quills. Cow appears perfectly well.

21st. No material change.

22d. Vesicle larger and more full, areola forming. Dipped several quills to-day; lymph pellucid. Drs. J. D. Fisher, C. Putnam and Gregerson examined the case to-day.

23d. Crust forming rapidly, areola somewhat increased in extent, three-fourths of an inch in diameter, round and regular, and somewhat raised above surrounding skin. Cow eats as usual. From this date disease rapidly subsided; a very dark crust was soon formed. On 27th, Drs. Fisher and Putnam brought me virus taken from a child vaccinated on the 21st instant, with the matter taken from this cow. The vesicle, as they both affirmed, exhibited the characteristic marks of the true cow-pox on the sixth day of the disease. Many persons were subsequently vaccinated with matter taken from this cow, and in every instance the true vaccine disease was the result.

This discovery of the identity, or rather, I should say, this proof of the identity of the vaccine and variolous diseases, is the most important fact observed in relation to the cow-pox, since the original discovery of Dr. Jenner. For if any doubt should ever arise as to the genuineness of the virus in use, or if it should at any time be lost, as it frequently may be in certain localities, and small-pox make its appearance, it can be reproduced with certainty by inoculating the cow with small-pox virus.

Much more evidence, if necessary, could be adduced from the writings of distinguished physicians, both in England, on the continent, and in our own country, to prove how groundless is the theory, that a deterioration has taken place in the efficiency of the vaccine virus in use at the present day; but I will not occupy your time any longer on this point, but pass to the consideration of the third assigned cause of the failure of the vaccine process, to protect against small-pox infection; which is, that the operation is not always perfectly performed: either the virus is taken at an improper time, or from an imperfectly developed vesicle, or is inserted into the arms of those who are otherwise so far diseased as to prevent its proper development.

In this cause, I have no doubt, we shall find a very prolific source of the evil complained of. A very able writer, in No. XIII. of the British and Forreign Medico-Chir. Review, uses the following language: "That the indiscriminate vaccination, which has been practised in this country (England) by ignorant and unqualified persons, with little or no regard to the condition of the subject, or to the character and progress of the vesicle formed, is to be regarded as one of the main causes of the frequent failure of the vaccine process, we are fully convinced." In our own country, from the mistaken notion that vaccination, however performed, affords complete immunity from small-pox infection, the performance of the operation very naturally, from its extreme simplicity, in many instances fell into the hands of ignorant and unprofessional persons, as schoolmasters, ministers, &c. Even fathers and mothers of families, setting aside the claims of experience and skill, conceived themselves competent to vaccinate their own children. Then, again, the saving of expense has, we have no doubt, led many to resort to this method of self-vaccination; and even among those who prefer to have the operation entrusted to competent hands, there is frequently a manifest unwillingness to remunerate the physician for any after examination into the character of the disease. Are we not, from this cause, sometimes almost forced to neglect the subsequent observation of the case? So long as so much looseness attaches to the operation, we must expect to see much impermanence of protection.

A schoolmaster, a minister, or a parent, may be competent to perform the simple operation of vaccination; but what can they be expected to know of the characteristics of the true disease, or how should they know when a vesicle is in the most perfect state for yielding a virus which would be sure to produce a true protective influence in another? And would they not be still less capable of judging when the recipient's state of health was such as to insure the most perfect development of the disease?

Are we not ourselves sometimes in fault in these matters? Are we always sufficiently cautious to draw our virus from none but perfect vesicles? Do we always observe accurately their anatomical development, and are we always informed in respect to the essential constitutional effects? And then, again, matter taken from a perfect vesicle at too late a period, will produce a spurious disease; pus will be so far mixed with the lymph as to produce, when introduced into the arm of another, an inflamed sore, and a pustule, which will exert but a very feeble if any protective influence on the recipient.

It is to be lamented that very respectable practitioners are too often careless in drawing their vaccine lymph from imperfectly developed cases, and also too negligent in watching the disease through its natural stages, so as to ascertain whether it passes through them perfectly. Hence so many cases in which the patient considers himself secure, when he is not so.

In England vaccination is more loosely done than here. Many vaccinate themselves, or have the operation performed by incompetent persons, who are regardless alike of the state of health of the recipient, and of the character of the vesicle and the physical condition of the person from whom the virus has been drawn. Mr. Marson, resident surgeon of the Small-pox and Vaccination Hospital, London, in the very able analytical examination made by him of all the cases admitted to that Hospital for sixteen years, says, that "the protective influence of vaccination varies in degree according as it has been perfectly or imperfectly performed." And in his letter to the Board of Health, published in their report made by order of government, he also shows that the danger of post-vaccinal small-pox is chiefly determined by the badness and insufficiency of their vaccination. He considers that the appearance of the cicatrices after a series of years, is the best evidence we can have of the perfection of vaccination. He describes a good vaccine cicatrix, as "distinct, foveated, dotted, or indented, in some instances radiated, and having a well, or tolerably well-defined edge." An indifferent cicatrix is "indistinct, smooth, without indentations, and with an irregular and ill-defined edge."

An able writer in a recent number of the British and Foreign Medico-Chirurgical Review, says: "We are rather inclined to ascribe any diminution of protective influence of the vaccine process, as due to personal carelessness in the selection of lymph, and the choice of cases, where lymph, for example, has been taken from a local vesicle developed in the absence of essential constitutional effect, and where not only the lymphy contents were impotent, but the anatomical development of the vesicle was at the same time incomplete or imperfect." Dr. Henry Ancell, of London, in reply to specific questions put by the General Board of Health, says: "One cause of imperfect vaccination is carelessness in the operation, by the use of foul or blunt instruments, producing an irritative wound, and modifying the specific influence by phlegmonous or erysipelatous inflammation. The vaccine vesicle runs a modified course; the lymph has a tendency to become quickly sero-purulent; the size, shape and tint of the areola present shades of difference obvious to a practised eye, but I believe often overlooked by the careless operator."

As a proof that vaccination should always be thoroughly and accurately performed in all its details, from the selection of the virus to the perfection of the disease, it is necessary only to refer to the army reports both of England and our own country. From the statistical report of Dr. Balfour upon the state of the British Army and Navy, where vaccination is always systematically performed, before the men are mustered into service, it appears that, during the eight years which the statistics cover, of the total number of soldiers (1,125,845), only 745 cases of small-pox occurred, or less than one-fifteenth of one per cent., or about one in 1550 persons; and among the whole number of sailors (363,370), there were 417 cases of small-pox; or about one in 900 persons. Also among the boys in the Military Asylum, who are all vaccinated, or have had small-pox, there have been 39 cases of small-pox and four deaths in 31,705 persons. It also appears that almost as many of these cases occurred in boys who had had small-pox, as among those who had been simply vaccinated. All the four deaths were in boys who had had small-pox. In the British army, vaccination is probably as accurately performed, in all its details, as in almost any other place on the globe. The result is, that less than one-fifteenth of one per cent. contract small-pox, and that in a very mild degree; while the subjects, on whom the observations were made, were frequently exposed to it under its most virulent forms, in all climates, and often under a strong epidemic influence.

The same is true in our own army. The regulation in regard to vaccination is very positive, and most rigidly enforced. Every recruit is vaccinated before he joins his regiment. The result is, as Dr. Porter, one of the Army Surgeons, in his surgical notes of the Mexican war, writes, that "in the whole course of my service in the regular regiments of the army, from the extreme North to the tropics, I have never seen a case of variola or varioloid in man, woman, or child; and the only cases of this disease I have ever seen, were among the irregular troops, and persons over whom we had no control."

We have examined the three causes usually assigned to account for the imperfect protection afforded by vaccination against small-pox infection. We have shown that the theories of the gradual elimination of the protective power of the disease by time, and the deterioration of the virus now in use, are entirely without foundation. And we have endeavored to show, not only by our own observations, but also by those of others, that it arises principally from the faulty and imperfect manner in which the operation has been too often performed.

There is no question that there are other circumstances which sometimes influence or alter the character and protective power of vaccination. For instance, if a child receives it while teething, or laboring under any disease, there is good evidence for the belief that the vaccine disease will often be very much more imperfect than if the operation had been performed when the child was in good health. Dr. Otto, an author already quoted, says: "From a very long and extensive practice, I am satisfied. that the agency of cow-pox virus may be counteracted, not only by fevers, and other pyrexial diseases, but also by a very nervous and irritable state of the body. The period of dentition is likewise unfavorable to its success." There are probably very few practitioners who have not experienced difficulty in producing the disease effectually under these circumstances; and should they be so indiscreet as to take matter from persons·thus vaccinated, it would not always produce the most perfect development of the disease in another.

The susceptibility to small-pox appears also to be increased during certain periods of an individual's life. This increased susceptibility seems not to be so much due to any deterioration or ·elimination of the protective power of the vaccine disease, as to some physiological changes which take place in the system during the period of maturation, for after this process has been completed, the susceptibility disappears, and the original "protectedness," as it is sometimes called, of the individual, becomes reestablished. I cannot better express this fact than by quoting Dr. Marson's statement. I will remark that Dr. Marson is the Resident Surgeon of the· Small-pox and Vaccination Hospital, London; and that his observations are founded on many thousand cases of which he has kept accurate notes. His. statement reads thus: "But few patients under ten years of·age have been received with small-pox after

33

vaccination. After ten years the number begins to increase considerably, and the largest admitted are from the decennial period from the age of fifteen to twenty-five; and, although progressively diminishing, they continue rather large up to thirty; and from thirty to thirty-five, they are nearly the same as from ten to fifteen; but as in the unprotected, at this period of life, the *mortality* is doubled, showing the cause to be, probably, as much or more depending on age and its concomitants as on other circumstances. In still further advanced life, the rate of mortality will be seen to increase also, as in the unprotected state; but this tendency may be in a considerable degree counteracted, there is but little doubt, by giving more attention than has hitherto generally been given to the perfection of the process of vaccination." We cannot suppose that the protective power of the vaccine disease is in any way suspended during this period of life, and then renewed at its expiration. We should rather believe that during this active stage of all the physical powers, the protection for the time was partially over-ridden, or, in other words, that during this stage of physical activity, the early vaccination was insufficient to keep pace with such rapid development, but at maturity it again assumed its control, and the original equilibrium was re-established. A re-vaccination at the age of ten or twelve would, in all probability, cover the increased susceptibility incident to this period of active physical development.

The protective power of the vaccine process appears also to be influenced by the number of vesicles. Some recent observations go to show, that the protective power of this disease is somewhat in proportion to the number of vesicles formed in the individual; and it is alleged that the constitutional effect is also in the same ratio. Mr. Marson noted the protective effect by the number of cicatrices. Thus, of those who had small-pox after vaccination, and showed but one cicatrix, 7 1-2 per cent died; of those with two cicatrices, the mortality was 4 per cent; those with three cicatrices, the average mortality was 1 3-4 per cent.; and of those who had four cicatrices, the average mortality was only 3-4 of one per cent. Others have observed similar facts, which seem to prove that the susceptibility is diminished as the number of cicatrices is increased. Should we not then establish the prophylactic power of the disease more perfectly if we uniformly introduced into the system, by an increased number of punctures, more of the vaccine matter than is usually thought to be sufficient simply to produce an outward development of the disease? There is no question, in my mind, that the degree of protection, which every one experiences from vaccination, is in exact proportion to the specific constitutional effect produced.

There is scarcely a doubt that something of the kind is true of small-pox. From the limited observations I have been able to make, it appears to me there is strong presumptive evidence, though not amounting to positive proof, that those who receive small-pox by inoculation are not as perfectly protected from a subsequent attack of the same, as those who take it in the natural way. When it is re-

ceived into the system in the latter manner, we know
it is much more virulent, the pocks are more numer-
ous, and the constitutional disturbance is much
greater, than when it is produced by inoculation.
Is not this to be accounted for, on the ground that
a much smaller amount of the poison is introduced
in this artificial mode of producing the disease, than
finds its way into the system when small-pox is contracted by freely breathing an infected atmosphere?
Yet sufficient poison, in the former instance, is introduced to cover, in a great majority of instances,
all subsequent liability to the disease, except perhaps under strong predisposing circumstances.

It is not my purpose, on this occasion, to enter
upon the discussion of the question of the relative
amount of disease produced by inoculation, as it is
now performed, compared with the same disease produced by direct exposure to its contagious influence.
I have only thrown out the hint, in the hope
that some one may give to the subject the investigation which its importance demands.

Is post-vaccinal small-pox relatively any more frequent, in fact, than small-pox after inoculation?
Our observations have led us to the conclusion that when, from the examination of the
cicatrices, there is good evidence that vaccination
has been properly performed, it is not comparatively any more frequent, than second small-pox.
It should be remembered that with us, at the present
day, the opportunities of observing secondary small-
pox are very limited, from the fact that there are
comparatively very few persons who have had the

primary disease. A careful examination, however, of the writings of others on the subject, from the time of Jenner to the present day, conclusively shows this statement to be true. I have time to refer, very briefly, to a few only of these authorities.

Dr. Ring, who wrote on cow-pox near the commencement of the present century, conclusively proves that second small-pox is very far from being rare. He does not, however, draw any comparison as to the relative frequency of this and post-vaccinal small-pox. But a report on this subject was made to this Society, in 1808, by a distinguished member,* who at the end of half a century from that day, honors us by his presence at this anniversary, in which he comes to the conclusion, that persons who undergo the cow-pox are thereby rendered as incapable of being affected by the virus of small-pox, as if they had undergone the latter disease. Dr. Barron, in his report on vaccination, made to the Provincial Medical and Surgical Association, says, " the cases of small-pox occurring after vaccination are scarcely, on the whole, more in number than those occurring after a previous attack of small-pox, and the resulting mortality so small, in the partially protected cases, as to be of little or no account in the general mass."

Sir Henry Halford, President of the Royal College of Physicians, in an official report made to the home department of his own government, uses the following language:—" Of an equal number of per-

---

* This report was nominally made by a committee, but was understood to be the work of the chairman, Dr. James Jackson.

sons *vaccinated and inoculated*, only so many of the former will be capable of taking the small-pox afterwards, and that in a safe degree of the disease, as are found to die of the latter." That is, as many will die of small-pox received by inoculation, as will take small-pox after vaccination.

Small-pox by inoculation is not, then, a perfect protection against a recurrence of the disease ; and when it does appear a second time, it is often violent in character, and not unfrequently fatal in its result. Instances have indeed occurred where persons have died from a third and even a fourth attack of it. On the other hand, it must be admitted that there are those who do not receive perfect protection from vaccination ; but if small-pox appears in these partially protected cases, it is in a very mild form, and comparatively of very little moment.

We are inevitably brought to the conclusion that the protective power of the vaccine disease is the same now as at any former period of its history, and that any apparent deviation from this, which may have, from time to time, shown itself in the more frequent occurrence of small-pox after vaccination, is not to be attributed to any deterioration in the agent itself, but to the neglect of proper care in its application.

How is this want of proper care in the application of the vaccine virus to be obviated ? We shall very briefly enumerate some of the more prominent means which have occurred to us.

1st. None but persons properly qualified should be allowed to perform vaccination. This, I am aware, is not under the direct control of the profession. Individual members can do no more than advise the employment, in all instances, of persons fully competent to perform the operation, and point out the evil consequences of deviations from this course.

2d. Every physician, when called upon to perform vaccination, should make it a part of his duty always to examine each case, as often as may be necessary, to satisfy himself that the disease has been properly developed. To enable him to do this, he should consider this attention to the progress of each case, as coming under the head of professional services; if we treat the subject as one of importance, the people will soon learn to take the same view of it.

3d. Great care should always be exercised to take the virus from none but perfectly developed vesicles, possessing the characteristics of the true vaccine disease. To this end, physicians should study thoroughly the natural history of the disease, and accurately observe it through all its stages; they should watch carefully the anatomical development of the little cells, which indicate, more certainly perhaps than any other one thing, the true character of the vesicle.

4th. The existing state of health, and the age of the person, have much to do with the proper development of the vesicle. When these are at any time in fault, a re-vaccination should be resorted to at the earliest practicable period.

5th. Number of vesicles. It has been shown,

that those persons who have three or more cicatrices are more perfectly protected, than those who have but one. In this country, we have generally been satisfied if we produced but one, or at most two good vesicles. Many high authorities recommend not less than three, and some even more than that. In the present state of our knowledge, we should hardly be satisfied with less than three well developed vesicles. Then, again, it is a question, whether the protection ordinarily afforded to the individual may not be impaired by drawing the virus from these vesicles. It certainly should not be taken from more than one of them. These are questions of great importance, as has already been shown, and certainly require more accurate investigation than has yet been bestowed upon them.

On the question of frequent or occasional re-vaccination, Dr. Marson, in the paper from which we have already repeatedly·quoted, says, " It probably does not afford the same amount of protection that the first vaccination, well performed, does. The great object to aim at is, to vaccinate *well* in infancy. This should be looked upon as the sheet anchor; and therefore a careless vaccination should be deprecated at all times, practised under the belief that if it fails to take effect properly, it will be of no consequence, as the operation can be repeated. By such proceeding, the vaccination often takes effect *badly*, and will never afterwards take effect *properly*."

Our own observations have led us to the following conclusions, viz.: that it is of the utmost importance that the first vaccination should be performed with great care ; that if the susceptibility to receive small-pox is once extinguished in the system, it remains so, and re-vaccination is superfluous. In order that we may be sure that this susceptibility is extinguished, vaccination should be repeated so long as it produces any specific effect; especially should it always be repeated when the first operation has been performed at an early age, during dentition, or when disease of any kind, or a diseased diathesis, existed. Then, as so much looseness in the manner of performing vaccination, and in the selection of the virus, has been shown to exist, it would be well always, as a matter of precaution, to re-vaccinate all who may at any time be directly exposed to small-pox. If this be done, on or before the fifth day after exposure, it will usually take precedence of, or essentially modify, that disease. This precautionary measure would, we believe, be entirely unnecessary, could we be perfectly satisfied that the above prerequisites had been strictly observed.

Gentlemen, I have, as briefly as circumstances would allow, presented to you the result of my investigation of certain questions in relation to the vaccine disease. Other questions of equal importance demand further examination, but could not be brought within the compass of this address. I trust some more able hands will perform this service.

I cannot conclude this discourse without an allusion to the events of the past year. Each of these anniversaries brings fresh accessions to our fraterni-

34

ty, and reminds us of others whose work is done. Since our last meeting, some, who cheered us then by their presence, have ceased from labor among the living. Some in ripe and honored age; some in the meridian of life and successful duty; others at the threshold of a career, bright with hope and promise to themselves and others. They have laid down the armor; we wear it still. May their example stimulate us to renewed efforts to alleviate the sufferings of humanity, and to prepare ourselves for that change which awaits us all; so that when we are called upon to bow before disease, from which it has been the labor of our lives to rescue our fellow beings, we may be able to do it with submission and hope, and leave examples worthy to cheer and guide those who enter into our labors.